Everything On The Farm Poops

by Kelly Lee Culbreth

Illustrated by Danh Fran Art

Kelly Lee Culbreth is a Midwestern girl who never paid much attention to the cattle, corn and soybean fields growing up – until her sister married a farmer! After years of observing her growing family, Kelly learned the farm can be a surprising place, where family comes together with love, laughter and hard work. Although this book flows with humor and promises a good laugh, you will also learn about the purpose of that stinky stuff on the farm! ENJOY!

Dedicated in memory of William Lee Culbreth.

I dedicate this book to my late father. He told me I could do anything I wanted to do, and be anything I wanted to be. His inspiration gave me the courage to see this project through and to dream big.
My Dad had a GREAT sense of humor,
and I know he would have LOVED this book!

Don't just be a Dreamer... be a Doer!
~ Kelly Lee Culbreth

Hi! My name is Kelly, I have a story to tell.
It's about something yucky, and stinky as well.
I made a discovery the other day...
Why my Home & the Farm differ in a big way.

See... when you live in the town or in the city,
all the streets and yards look oh-so-pretty.
The sidewalk is a safe place to stroll,
as no animals use it like a toilet bowl.

But when I visit family in Southern Illinois,
there's a barn full of animals and lots of land to enjoy.
And when I see the cows and chicken coops,
I quicky learn that... Everything On The Farm Poops!

There are goats and chickens and pigs who get muddy.
There's even a friendly pet cow named Buddy.
There's dogs and cats and horses too,
but all of these animals have to go POO!
The bigger the animal, the bigger the pile.
When it hits the ground, you can see them smile.

They ate a good meal their tummy pushed through.
And then their belly turned that food into poo.
So when on the farm, you must watch where you walk,
or you will step in a big stinky shock!
Some call it dookie, scat, dung or stool.
But the farmers see fertilizer in that cow manure.

I promise this book won't lose its charm,
as I tell stories of my visit to the farm.
With lots to do and daily chores,
there's always a surprise behind those barn doors.

So go get your shovel and wheelbarrow, too.
`Cause the horses and cows left lots of brown goo.
Make sure to gather all that is found,
for we need that poo to feed the ground.
I know that cow poop is stinky and gross,
but it's just what the farm is needing the most.

You see... poop has a purpose, and this I know.
Because without it, the garden and crops won't grow!
Manure is chewed-up grass and grain,
with organic nutrients the plants will retain.
Once spread on the ground with seeds and straw, too,
we'll grow food we can eat to turn back into poo.

Now after their chores, the kids like to play.
And then sweet Kaolin has something to say.
"Hey, watch your step," she says to the group.
"Because last week, that's where my dog pooped."
I said, "Don't worry, I doubt it's still there."
But just to be sure, we looked everywhere.

Then she asked, "Why can't it be found?"
I answered, "Remember? Poop's food for the ground."
The kids laughed and said, "Ew, that's gross!"
Then little Porter made a funny joke.
"With all our animals that run free,
our yard will never, ever go hungry!"

Why yes, the farm is covered in goo.
And even the sky has clouds shaped like poo.
The sun's going down, but there's work left to do.
The cows need to be fed and the family, too.
You can smell dinner cooking inside of the kitchen.
And those who like baking, decided to pitch in.

Then Grandpa yells out, "Time to head to the pasture.
The cows need to eat and with help it goes faster."
"Oh count me in!" little Parker says.
"I love to feed the cows before bed!"
"Well grab your boots, we need to work steady.
I want to get done before dinner is ready."

Now here is where the fun gets started,
as Grandpa and Grandson together departed.
They mixed a batch full of grass, hay and corn,
to load into feeders that look fully worn.
Thank goodness for boots that are sure to get muddy,
from walking through fields that are soft just like putty

But don't look down, `cause if you do...
You'll see an obstacle course made of poo!
There's piles and piles in all different sizes.
So don't be surprised when a smell arises!
To farmers, the odor is no big deal.
But us city folk think there is NO appeal.

Our farmers walk in from feeding the cattle.
They better clean up so there won't be a battle.
Grandpa heads to the shower to get squeaky clean
But Parker climbs on the chair just to be seen.
"Step away from the table, you're covered in dirt.
There's mud on your pants and even your shirt."

"Nu-huh," he says, "oh, no it's not.
That's not mud or dirt on me," he fought.
So just when it seems that I had been duped,
Parker yells out, "Because it's cow POOP!"
Well I stand corrected, but then I declared,
"Clean up or you can't eat this meal we prepared."

14

The food was yummy, we scarfed it down.
and then we heard a funny sound....

At first it got quiet, then we started to giggle.
Because Grandma looked guilty, as we watched her wig
"I'm sorry," she said, "wish that had been muted.
That clatter you heard was me when I tooted."
The kids held their noses, 'cause they all knew,
that when Grandma was gassy, the smell was Pee-Ye

Then off she went to use the restroom.
`Cause a toot meant #2 would come soon.
Now why didn't Grandma just go poo-poo outside?
Since the animals seem to do it all the time?
Well, all their poop helps the ground stay fertilized.
But for humans to do it, it's just plain uncivilized!

Yeah, humans and animals are different for sure.
We can talk, walk upright and have no fur.
But one special difference I must point out,
involves a question to think about:
"How come when animals go poo,
they don't need any toilet tissue?"

Well, I thought, they probably do.
But how do you wipe with a hoof or horseshoe?
Their arms won't reach, even if they tried.
They can barely touch their underside.
Besides, I bet they don't even mind,
when they have a little doo-doo left on their behind!

18

Although I love visiting family and friends,
all visits to the farm must come to an end.
But this city girl leaves with memories to share,
about all the stinky things I saw there.

Making kids laugh and adults too,
is easy with jokes about toots and poo.
One way to do this without jumping through hoops,
s tell stories on how... Everything on the Farm Poops!

How many P😊😊PS are on each page?

Page 1 _____   Page 6 _____   Page 11 _____   Page 16 _____

Page 2 _____   Page 7 _____   Page 12 _____   Page 17 _____

Page 3 _____   Page 8 _____   Page 13 _____   Page 18 _____

Page 4 _____   Page 9 _____   Page 14 _____   Page 19 _____

Page 5 _____   Page 10 _____   Page 15 _____   Page 20 _____

Where is Willow?

Kelly's dog, Willow, appears 7 times in the book. Can You Find Her?

#1 _____

#2 _____

#3 _____

#4 _____

#5 _____

#6 _____

#7 _____

Made in the USA
Las Vegas, NV
04 October 2022

56534634R00017